I'm Tyrannosaurus!

A Book of Dinosaur Rhymes

ISBN 0-590-44641-X

Text copyright © 1993 by Jean Marzollo.
Illustrations copyright © 1993 by Hans Wilhelm, Inc.
All rights reserved. Published by Scholastic Inc.
CARTWHEEL BOOKS™ is a trademark of Scholastic Inc.

12 11 10 9 8 7 6 5 4 3   5 6 7 8/9

Printed in the U.S.A.   24

First Scholastic printing, September 1993

I'm Tyrannosaurus!

A Book of Dinosaur Rhymes

by Jean Marzollo • Illustrated by Hans Wilhelm

Cartwheel
·B·O·O·K·S· ®

SCHOLASTIC INC.
New York   London   Toronto   Sydney   Auckland

Tyrannosaurus Rex

Tie-ran-uh-SOR-us REX
"Tyrant Lizard"

I'm Tyrannosaurus!
I've got it made;
With my long, sharp teeth,
I'm never afraid.

Diplodocus

Dip-PLOD-uh-cus
"Double Beam"

I am Diplodocus,
Gigantic and slow;
I like to eat plants
Wherever I go.

Leptopterygius

Lep-toe-ter-IDGE-ee-us
"Partially Finned"

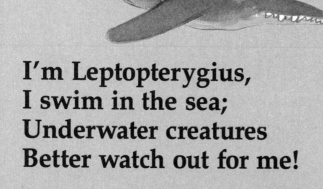

I'm Leptopterygius,
I swim in the sea;
Underwater creatures
Better watch out for me!

Stegosaurus

Steg-uh-SOR-us
"Plated Lizard"

I'm Stegosaurus,
Big as a whale,
With plates on my back
And spikes on my tail.

Ankylosaurus

An-KY-luh-SOR-us
"Stiffened Lizard"

I'm Ankylosaurus
With spikes on my back
And a club-like tail —
Ready, aim, smack!

Triceratops

Try-SAIR-uh-tops
"Three-horned Face"

I'm Triceratops,
With horns and a beak
And a collar-like frill
That is rather unique.

Quetzalcoatlus

Ket-sol-ko-AT-lus
Named after Quetzalcoatl,
the Aztec winged
serpent god

I'm Quetzalcoatlus,
A reptile in the sky;
I haven't any feathers,
But I still can fly.

Coelophysis
See-low-FICE-sis
"Hollow Form"

I'm Coelophysis,
Swift and small,
I'm one of the oldest
Dinosaurs of all.

Saltopus

SAWL-tuh-puss
"Leaping Foot"

I'm little Saltopus
And I've been taught
If you don't run away,
You're gonna get caught!

Anatosaurus

An-at-uh-SOR-us
"Duck Lizard"

I'm Anatosaurus,
No big thrill,
Just a "dinosaur duck"
With a funny flat bill.

Protoceratops

Pro-to-SER-uh-tops
"First Horned Face"

I'm Protoceratops
On four squat legs;
Like other dinosaurs,
I lay eggs.

Pteranodon

Ter-AN-uh-don
"Winged and Toothless"

I am Pteranodon,
I love to glide;
With my ten-foot wings
I can soar and slide.

Iguanodon

Ig-WAN-uh-don
"Iguana Tooth"

I am Iguanodon;
I sit on a seat
Which is really my tail
And can't be beat.

Brachiosaurus

Brack-ee-o-SOR-us
"Arm Lizard"

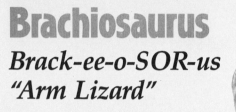

I'm Brachiosaurus —
Biggest of all;
I weigh 80 tons
And I'm four stories tall!

Facts About Dinosaurs

- All the facts stated in these poems are true, but in this book there are two kinds of pictures — real and imaginary. Can you tell which is which? The imaginary pictures (the big ones) will help you remember the facts about the animals in the small pictures.
- The word "dinosaur" means "terrible lizard."
- Dinosaurs lived millions of years ago — long before people lived on the earth.
- Dinosaurs are extinct, which means that they all died out. There are no more dinosaurs today.
- Some dinosaurs ate plants, and some ate meat.
- Leptopterygius, pteranodon, and quetzalcoatlus were not dinosaurs, but they lived at the same time as the dinosaurs.
- If you like to study dinosaurs, maybe you'll be a paleontologist when you grow up. A paleontologist is a dinosaur scientist.
- Paleontologists dig up dinosaur bones. The bones have turned into stones called fossils. Paleontologists assemble the bones into dinosaur skeletons to study. You can see some of these skeletons in dinosaur museums.